Bamboo & Friends

The Furry Caterpillar

by Felicia Law
illustrated by Claire Philpott,
Karen Radford, and Xact Studio

Editor: Jill Kalz
Page Production: Brandie E. Shoemaker
Creative Director: Keith Griffin
Editorial Director: Carol Jones

First American edition published in 2007 by
Picture Window Books
5115 Excelsior Boulevard
Suite 232
Minneapolis, MN 55416
877-845-8392
www.picturewindowbooks.com

Printed in the United States of America.

Library of Congress Cataloging-in-Publication Data
Law, Felicia.
The furry caterpillar / by Felicia Law ; illustrated by
Claire Philpott, Karen Radford, and Xact Studio.
p. cm. — (Bamboo & friends)
Summary: Bamboo, Velvet, and Beak receive a big surprise
when Bamboo's furry pillow turns out not to be a pillow at all.
ISBN-13: 978-1-4048-2599-4 (hardcover)
ISBN-10: 1-4048-2599-1 (hardcover)
[1. Caterpillars—Fiction. 2. Rain forest animals—Fiction.]
I. Philpott, Claire, ill. II. Radford, Karen, ill. III. Xact
(Firm : Delhi, India) IV. Title. V. Series: Law, Felicia.
Bamboo & friends.
PZ7.L41835Fur 2006
[E]—dc22   2006012129

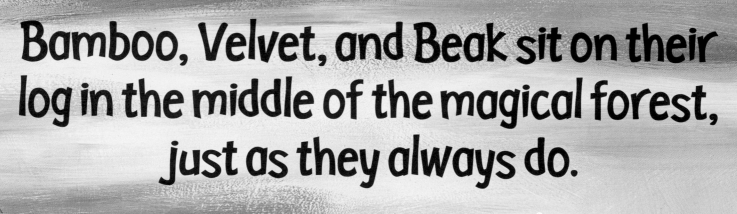

Bamboo, Velvet, and Beak sit on their log in the middle of the magical forest, just as they always do.

"Have you two seen my egg?" asks Beak. "I put it right over here. I was going to eat it for breakfast this morning."

"No," say Bamboo and Velvet together.

"Then what's that behind your head, Bamboo?" asks Beak.

"It's my pillow," says Bamboo.
"My furry pillow."

"That's not your furry pillow," says Beak. "That's MY furry caterpillar. It hatched out of MY egg. So it's still MY breakfast."

Caterpillars hatch from tiny eggs laid by butterflies.

7

"Pillows don't hatch from eggs,"
says Bamboo. "And you can't eat it.
It's soft and tickly. And it's mine."

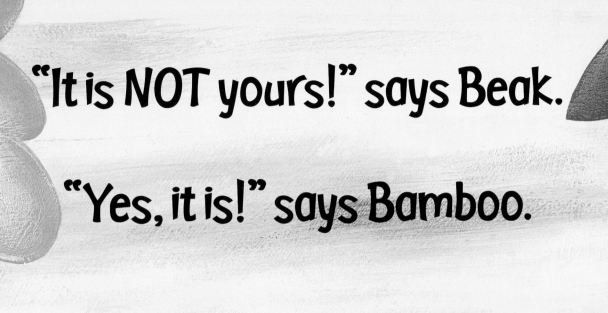

"It is NOT yours!" says Beak.

"Yes, it is!" says Bamboo.

9

"Your pillow seems to be very hungry,"
says Velvet. "All it does is eat."

Leaves are the main source of food for caterpillars.

Velvet is right. The pillow eats and eats. And it gets fatter and fatter ...

11

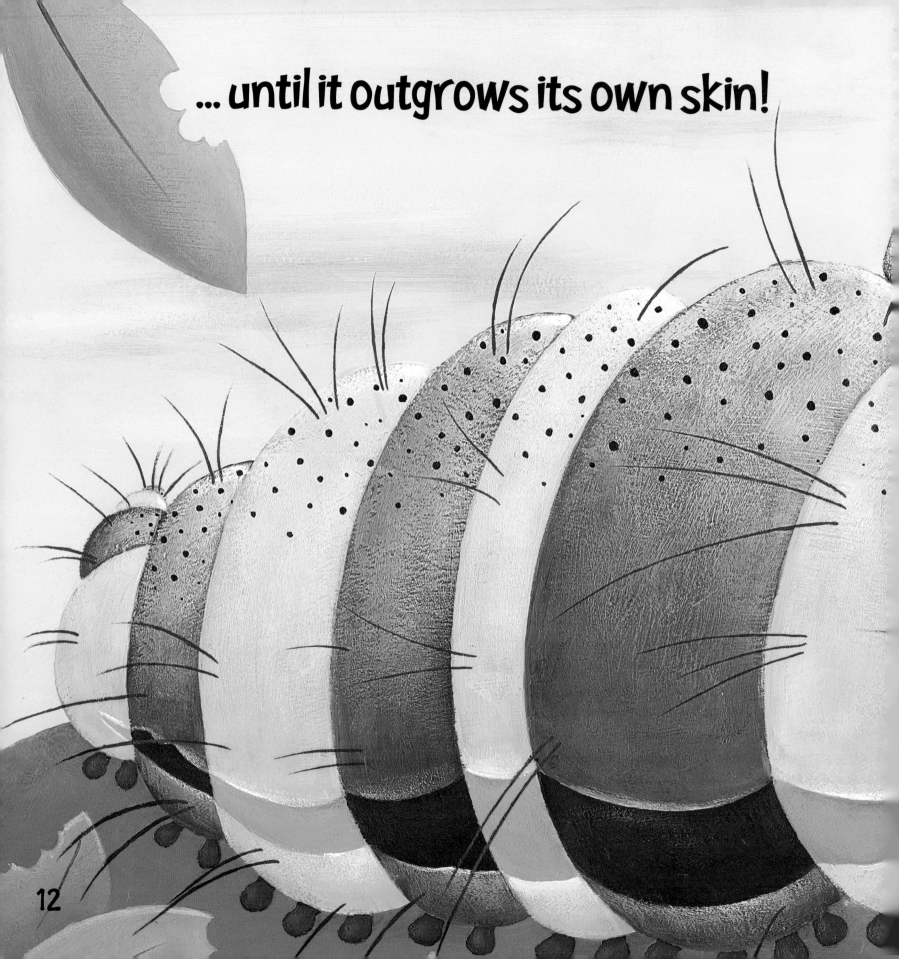

"Oops!" say
Bamboo, Velvet, and Beak.

13

An even larger furry caterpillar slides out of the split skin.

"My pillow got even bigger," says Bamboo.

"So did my breakfast," says Beak.

When an animal sheds its skin, feathers, or shell, it molts. Snakes, caterpillars, birds, and crabs are examples of animals that molt.

Every day, the caterpillar eats and eats. Every day, its skin splits, and an even larger caterpillar crawls out.

And every day, Bamboo and Beak argue.
Is it a big pillow or a big breakfast?
Velvet shakes her head and sighs.

When a caterpillar has grown to its full size, it makes a hard shell called a chrysalis.

Then one day the argument ends. Bamboo wakes up to find something hard under his head. "Where's my furry pillow?" he asks.

"Maybe it's hiding in that case," says Velvet. "Maybe it's tired of you and Beak arguing—just like I am!"

"Well, I don't want a hard pillow,"
says Bamboo. "You can have it, Beak."

Beak taps the shell. "It seems too
tough to eat now," he says.

"All shells are tough," says Velvet. "They help protect the soft stuff inside."

When a caterpillar is inside a chrysalis, it's called a pupa.

21

CRACK! CRACK! goes the shell.
It splits apart, and out flies a
beautiful butterfly!

"Goodbye!" it says. "I'm off to lay an egg!"

"Oh, dear!" says Velvet.
"It's going to start all over again!"

23

Fun Facts

- Caterpillars are capable of eating entire fields full of crops. A small group of caterpillars can quickly ruin a farmer's harvest.

- Some caterpillars are covered with long hair, while others have no hair at all.

- The hawk moth caterpillar has spots on it that look like snake eyes. These spots help scare away hungry birds.

- The word for more than one pupa is *pupae*.

- Just before a pupa hatches as a butterfly, its chrysalis becomes transparent, or see-through. Then the butterfly can be seen inside.

- Butterflies don't need as much food as caterpillars do. They aren't growing anymore, so they eat just for energy. Most butterflies eat nectar, a sweet liquid made by flowers.

- The Queen Alexandra's Birdwing is the largest butterfly in the world. With its wings open, it measures up to 12 inches (30.5 centimeters) across.

On the Web

FactHound offers a safe, fun way to find Internet sites related to this book. All of the sites on FactHound have been researched by our staff.

1. Visit **www.facthound.com**
2. Type in this special code for age-appropriate sites: 1404825991
3. Click on the FETCH IT button.

Your trusty FactHound will fetch the best sites for you!

Look for all of the books in the Bamboo & Friends series: